Codi and the Maple Tree

written by Joseph Lauricella

illustrated by Olga Pietraszek

This book is dedicated to my
parents Edward and Jean Lauricella,
pack leaders who were always present and loving.

J.L.

Many years ago, on a sunny fall day, a timber wolf named Codi meandered his way through a dense forest. He was far from home and all alone on the northern most border of what is now Minnesota.

This was the land of the Chippewa people who were known for building canoes with birch tree bark. Timber wolves and the Chippewa people have been sharing the same land for thousands of years.

The leaves on the trees that were green all summer long changed into a colorful array. Red, yellow, pink, orange and purple leaves fell from their branches and covered the ground.

They crunched beneath Codi's paws as he trotted along the narrow stream.

Codi looked up and down a nearby hill and sniffed the air for clues. He was on a very important mission to find a new home for his family.

A late summer storm blew a tree down and it landed on his pack's den. There was a big hole in the roof where branches poked through and not enough room to move. His pack needed a new home before winter brought on the cold.

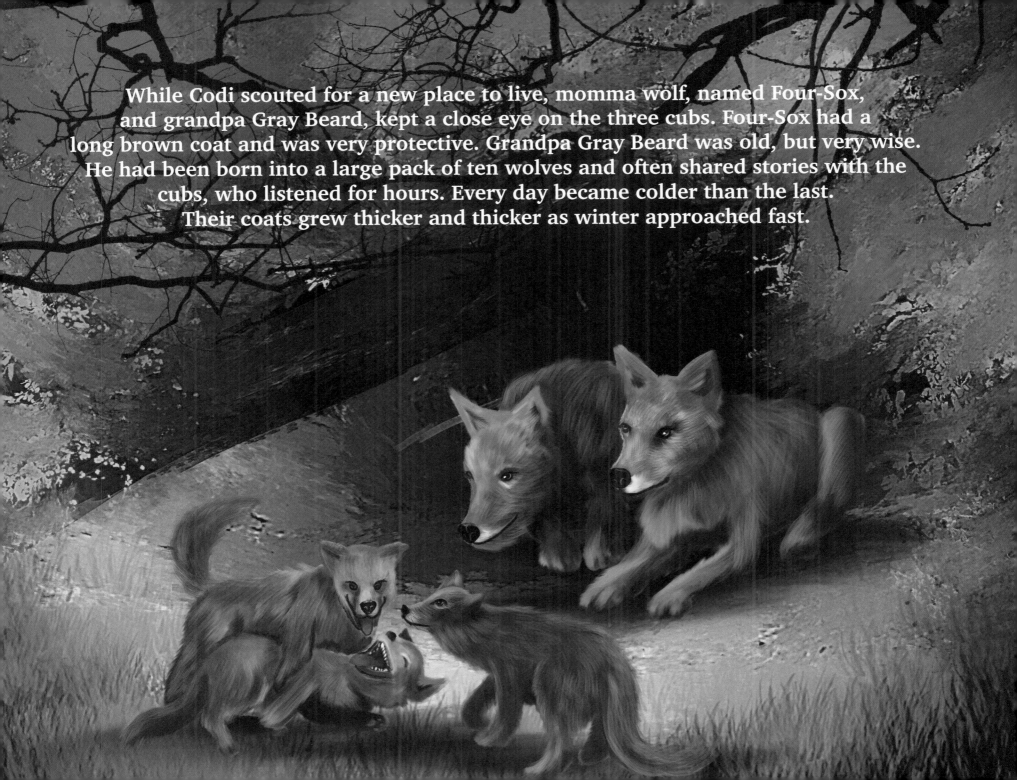

While Codi scouted for a new place to live, momma wolf, named Four-Sox, and grandpa Gray Beard, kept a close eye on the three cubs. Four-Sox had a long brown coat and was very protective. Grandpa Gray Beard was old, but very wise. He had been born into a large pack of ten wolves and often shared stories with the cubs, who listened for hours. Every day became colder than the last. Their coats grew thicker and thicker as winter approached fast.

Codi searched for weeks looking for the perfect place to dig a new den. Mile after mile, Codi grew more tired and hungry. He missed his pack, but he had to push on. He followed a stream and stopped at a fallen log and took a drink of the cool water. Just as he lifted his head, he saw the sun shining on a spot halfway up the hill. He leapt over the stream and dashed up the hill to scout it out.

Codi sniffed the ground, looked up and down, and listened closely to the sounds all around. He sat for a moment and sighed, knowing he had found the perfect place to dig a new den. The stream provided clean drinking water for the pack and the hillside offered protection from storms and intruders. Suddenly, Codi threw his head back and let out a howl.

"Owwwwwww!"

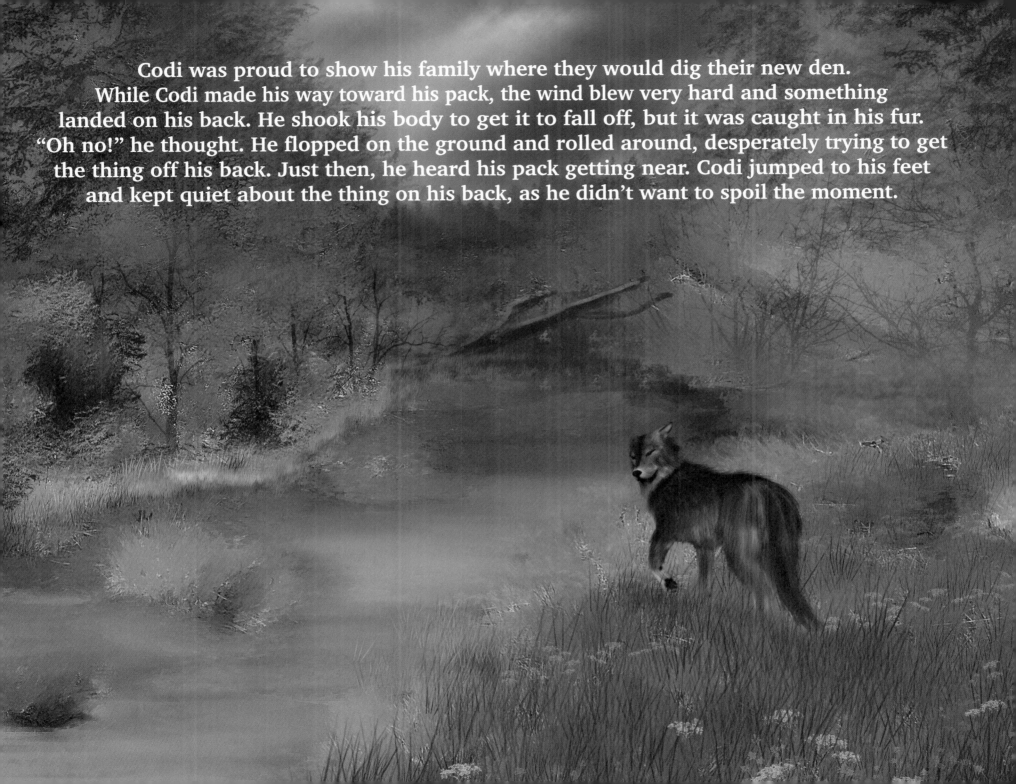

Codi was proud to show his family where they would dig their new den. While Codi made his way toward his pack, the wind blew very hard and something landed on his back. He shook his body to get it to fall off, but it was caught in his fur. "Oh no!" he thought. He flopped on the ground and rolled around, desperately trying to get the thing off his back. Just then, he heard his pack getting near. Codi jumped to his feet and kept quiet about the thing on his back, as he didn't want to spoil the moment.

The pack was excited to see the place for the new den, but Gray Beard stood alone on a large rock sniffing the air and looking up at the sky. He knew a winter storm was approaching and they needed to take shelter in their old den. They would have to wait until spring to see their new home.

It was a long, hard winter that year, with short days and little light. Codi foraged through the long cold nights despite that irritating thing hurting his back more and more every day. Some days he could barely even run. If he couldn't hunt, the pack might starve. He had to bring food home to the cubs—no matter what.

One day while the cubs were nestled in, Codi hobbled over to Grandpa Gray Beard and told him about his hurting back.

"Codi, you're a strong smart wolf, but to be a good leader you must learn to ask for help when you need it." As Gray Beard trotted off, Codi sat alone in the melting snow to think about grandpa's advice.

The warmth of spring finally arrived and the wolves began shedding their coats. They rubbed against trees and rocks scratching each other's backs with play. All of a sudden, Codi let out a big howl.

"Owwwwwwww!"

The cubs came running over and stood at attention.

Codi said, "I have something stuck in my fur and it has been hurting my back all winter long. Can you please help me get it out?"

The cubs took turns scratching Codi's back. They scratched and scratched and pulled and nibbled on Codi's dense coat. As clumps of fur blew in the wind, little birds swooped down and carried some away.

After many swipes of their paws and claws, the thing finally broke free from his back. All this time, Codi had a seedpod from a maple tree stuck deep in his fur! The pack erupted with great big happy howls. "Owwwwwwwwww! Owwwwwwwww!"

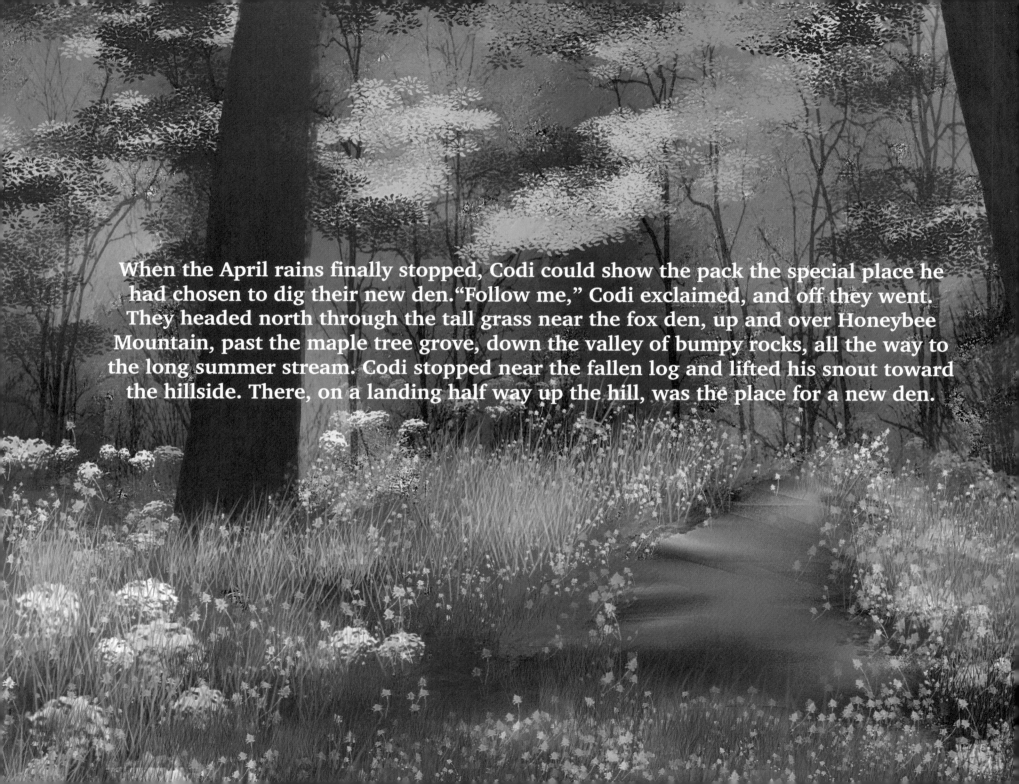

When the April rains finally stopped, Codi could show the pack the special place he had chosen to dig their new den. "Follow me," Codi exclaimed, and off they went. They headed north through the tall grass near the fox den, up and over Honeybee Mountain, past the maple tree grove, down the valley of bumpy rocks, all the way to the long summer stream. Codi stopped near the fallen log and lifted his snout toward the hillside. There, on a landing half way up the hill, was the place for a new den.

"Who is ready to dig our new den?" Codi asked. All at once the cubs lifted their snouts, opened their mouths, and let out a howl.

"Owwwww! Ow Ow Owwwww!"

All afternoon the cubs dug and dug, high on the hill in the land of the Chippewa people. When the den was free from all the roots and rocks and big enough for the entire pack, the cubs sprawled out and fell asleep one by one.

While the wolf pack was busy making their new den, they had forgotten about the seedpod.

Mother nature had not forgotten. Her rain had washed it away until it became lodged under a little rock.

That summer, the seedpod from Codi's fur grew roots
that entered the ground and a new maple tree was born.

Many years have gone by now. Codi and Four-Sox had two more litters of cubs and their children had their own litters, but that maple tree still stands strong in the same spot where the rain washed the seedpod down.

On hot summer days, children play and swing under the shade of the maple tree. And sure enough, every fall just before the first snow, a howl is heard from high on the hill. It just might be a descendant of Codi's pack looking for the maple tree planted long ago.